Rebecca's Daughter

Siân Lewis

Illustrated by Graham Howells

Rebecca's Daughter

Mam was wailing at the top of her voice. I heard her when I was cutting thistles in the field. It scared me so much, I dropped my sickle and ran home as fast as I could.

'Oh, my poor children!' she was shouting. 'My poor children. It's the workhouse for us all!'

I thought the cart had come to take us to the workhouse. Last year it came to fetch Annie Blaenpant, because she had no money and no food. You should have heard Annie and her seven children crying and bawling as they were taken off to that cold, cruel place.

I ran so fast I slipped on the muck in the lane and went bowling like a stone up to our door.

'Lizzie, Lizzie,' called my father. 'Are you all right?'

'All right?' cried my mother. 'How can you expect the poor child to be all right?'

I picked myself up and rubbed my knee. 'What's wrong now?' I said with a sigh. There was no sign of trouble after all. It was only Mam making a fuss. My little brothers were sitting on the doorstep and Mam and Dad were down by the hen house.

'It's your father!' said Mam, flinging back her head. 'He's only going to ruin us all.'

I looked at Dad. He gave me a wink that Mam didn't see.

'He's only going to get us sent to the workhouse,' wailed Mam.

There was a screech from my brother Will. Though he's only five years old, he's the eldest of my brothers. My parents had five girls followed by three boys. I am thirteen and the eldest of all of us. Will ran to Mam and buried his face in her skirts.

'You're scaring him with all your talk,' my father said.

'Scaring him with my talk, am I?' said Mam. 'So what happens when he really gets hauled off to the workhouse? What happens then?'

Will screeched again. Isaac ran up to see what was wrong and Johnnie came crawling very fast through the middle of the hens. Mam picked up Johnnie and hugged him so hard he squealed like a rat.

By then I had guessed why Mam was making a fuss. Dad wanted to join the Daughters of Rebecca again. He was going to smash the tollgate.

Mam hates the tollgate, mind. We all do. We hate to see it blocking our road. Each time we take the cart out, we have to pay to go through the tollgate at Efail-wen. When we go to fetch lime, it costs us three whole pence which we can't afford. That's why the local men got together to smash down the tollgate one week after it was put up last May. They weren't caught because they'd all dressed up as women and rubbed soot on their faces so no one would recognise them. I knew who one of them was, though. My dad.

That night Dad had come home late. When I lifted my head from the mattress, I saw him drop a large bundle on the floor. I had a look at the bundle in the morning. It

was a heap of Mam's clothes. I couldn't understand what her clothes were doing there, till I heard about the smashed tollgate and the Daughters of Rebecca. The men who smash the tollgates call themselves Rebecca's Daughters, because of a verse in the Bible which says that the children of Rebecca will 'possess the gate of those which hate them.'

Mam didn't shout at Dad that day in May, even though those clothes had sooty marks on them. In fact I heard her singing and laughing as she washed her clothes in the brook and spread them on the hedge to dry. She wasn't angry when the tollgate was smashed on the sixth of June either. On that night there was such a noise we could hear it from our place. Hundreds of people had rushed at the tollgate. There were seven constables there too, but they didn't stand a chance. They were chased away like scared rabbits. It was a clear night and I saw one of them go flying across the field below us with half his clothes torn off. Mam was with me and we both laughed and cheered.

Mam wasn't scared then. It's the talk of soldiers that's scared her. Three weeks ago there were soldiers marching around Narberth with their bayonets at the ready. On a Sunday too! Those stuck-up people who are justices of the peace had sent for them, because they were afraid that more gates would be wrecked. As well as smashing the gate at Efail-wen, the Daughters of Rebecca have smashed the gate at Maesgwyn.

'Your dad,' said Mam in a warbling voice – she's good at doing a warbling voice – 'is going to get sent to prison and where will we be then?'

'In the workhouse!' wailed Will.

'Workhouth,' mumbled Isaac through his thumb.

'I won't be caught,' said Dad. 'And I won't be sent to prison.'

'That's what you think,' said Mam. 'Some of the men got caught at Maesgwyn, didn't they? And they got sent to prison.'

'But…' Dad sighed and bit his tongue. In fact all the men who'd been caught at Maesgwyn had been let out of prison, because no one would give evidence against them.

'Oh my poor children. My poor mites,' moaned Mam. 'What will become of us?'

'But what will become of us, if we keep on paying tolls?' said Dad. 'It's hardly worth taking our eggs to market. And anyway that Thomas Bullin had no right to put up the new gate at Efail-wen. It's us that have got the right to take it down. And I can't just sit at home and let the other men do the dirty work for me. It wouldn't be fair.'

'We'll say you've been injured,' said Mam, quick as a flash. 'Lizzie can take the cart out tomorrow. She can tell everyone.'

I looked at Dad. My dad looked at me. I felt sorry for him but I said nothing. I didn't want to go to the workhouse.

But then I didn't want to pay at the tollgate either.

We haven't always had to pay. The roads used to belong to everyone and everyone had to work to repair them. Now, in 1839, the roads belong to the Turnpike

9

Companies. Our road has been rented by Thomas Bullin. He gets all the toll money, so no wonder he's built a gate at Efail-wen and put his brother Benjamin in charge of it.

Next morning I was waiting at the tollgate before six o'clock. Old Jenkin was waiting there before me. I could hear his teeth chattering. Jenkin's land is worse than ours. You can hardly get a thing to grow there and he's all skin and bone.

Jenkin didn't ask why it was me driving the cart and not Dad. Twm Carnabwth did, though. Twm was next to arrive and his big voice boomed in my ear. 'So what are you doing here then, young Lizzie?'

'Dad can't walk,' I replied. 'He's hit his leg very bad.'

I had practised the lie so often, it sounded good, but Twm said, 'Oh he has, has he?' And when I looked round he had a disbelieving look in his eye.

'Yes, he has,' I said.

Just then Benjamin Bullin came to collect the tolls and Twm began shouting at him, so I paid up and tried to get away as fast as I could.

It was never going to be fast enough. Twm had caught up with me long before we got to the lime kiln at Ludchurch. He shouted, 'Lucky your dad has a strapping young daughter to do the work for him, eh?'

'Yes,' I said.

Twm insisted on coming with me to help load the lime onto the cart.

'I can do that,' I insisted.

'I'm sure you can,' he replied, as he shovelled the lime

11

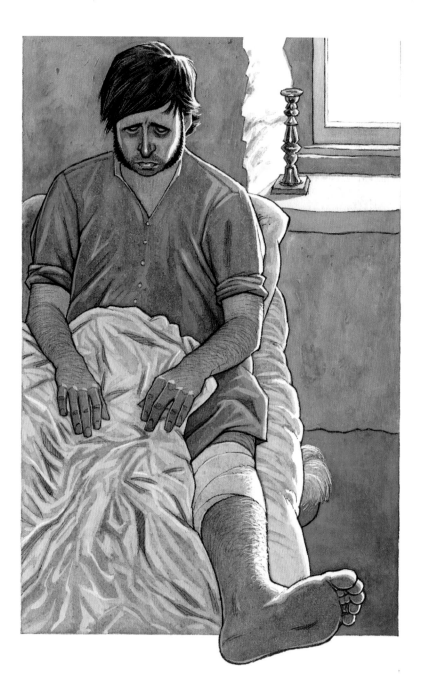

with his huge arms. 'But never let it be said that I didn't stop and help a friend in trouble. Your dad's in bed, is he?'

'Yes,' I said.

'Then tell him that Twm hopes he'll be better soon,' he said. 'Very soon.'

'Yes,' I said.

But I never said a word to Dad. I knew Twm didn't believe me and I didn't want Dad to know it. And by the way Twm said 'very soon', I guessed Rebecca and her Daughters would be on the move that night. I guessed Mam knew it too and that's why she'd made Dad stay at home.

I sneezed all the way home. The lime always gets into my throat and up my nose. There was lime in my cart. There was lime on the fields all around. There was lime everywhere. It looked as if it had been snowing. We have to put lime on our fields. Without it, nothing much will grow, because our land is so poor. Our land is poor. We are poor. So much of our money goes on rent and rates and tithes and now we have to pay at the tollgate. It's not fair!

When I got home, Dad was lying on his bed. Mam had made him stay there all morning. She'd even bandaged his leg to pretend he was hurt. Even by the dim light of our cottage I could see he looked miserable.

'Everything all right, Lizzie fach?' he asked.

'Yes,' I said.

'See anyone?'

'Old Jenkin,' I said, and dashed off to fetch the bread and buttermilk before he could ask any more questions.

Dad sighed a loud sigh that sounded like a gust of wind.

'Oh, stop that moaning, will you?' said Mam.

'But there's work to do, Maggie,' said Dad. 'I've got to make a start on the hay in Top Field.'

'Then I'll do it, won't I? Just as long as you promise to stay in that bed tonight.'

'Tonight?' said Dad.

'Yes,' said Mam with a very fierce look in her eye. 'Do you promise on the Bible not to go out tonight?'

We haven't got a Bible in the house, but Dad made a solemn promise all the same.

'I promise not to go out tonight,' he said.

I took the bread and buttermilk up to the potato field where my sisters were clearing the stones from the soil. The stones grow faster than potatoes in our field. Jane and Hannah were competing with Mary and Ellen to see who could make the biggest pile. But they soon came running when they saw the food. Jane had a big fat worm dangling from her grubby fingers. She would have swallowed it with her bread if I hadn't snatched it away.

We ate slowly and sat around till we saw Mam come out of the house with the scythe and head over the hill to Top Field. Then my sisters jumped up and went back to picking stones. I went down to get the cart, because it was my job to spread the lime on the thistle field.

I stopped off at the house to get a rag to wrap round my mouth and nose to stop me sneezing. Dad was sitting up

in bed. He gave me a fright. I wasn't used to seeing him there at that time of day and he was so still, I thought he was a statue.

'Are you all right?' I asked.

'No,' he said. 'I'm ashamed, Lizzie. Why should other people be putting themselves in danger for our sakes? I should be there with the Daughters of Rebecca tonight.'

'But you promised,' I said.

'Yes,' he replied.

My cheeks were prickling when I went outside and it wasn't because of the lime. Dad was right. It was cowardly of our family not to support Rebecca. I wished I'd been a boy then. Women are not allowed to be Daughters of Rebecca and my brothers are far too young. The three of them had gone up to the potato field and I could hear my sisters shouting at them not to mess up the piles of stones.

I hitched the horse on to the cart which bumped and rattled all the way across to the thistle field. I always count when I unload the lime. One, two, three, four, five shovelfuls. One, two, three, four, five shovelfuls. It stops me feeling tired and achy, because it gives my mind something to think about.

For once I didn't need to count. I didn't feel tired, because I couldn't stop thinking about Dad and the Daughters of Rebecca and the knowing look in Twm Carnabwth's eye. Twm Carnabwth is a boxer as well as a farmer. Dad is quite big, but Twm is much, much bigger. Twm would never be a coward. He'd never pretend he was ill just to get out of wrecking the gates. Well, Dad wasn't a

coward either. It wasn't fair if Twm thought so. Dad was only pretending to be ill, because he'd promised Mam.

'Dad isn't scared,' I said out loud and got a mouthful of rag for my trouble.

I had taken off the rag to rewind it, when I heard a noise. I suppose it had been going on for a while, but I'd been too busy to notice. It was the humming and drumming you hear when lots of cows are driven to market.

But it wasn't market day. I dropped my shovel and ran to the corner of the field where I could look down. A huge crowd was moving along the road below me. I had never seen so many shawls of all colours, nor seen so many swishing skirts. You would have thought it was a crowd of women. But it wasn't. These were the Daughters of Rebecca and they were moving around in broad daylight.

At the head of the crowd was Rebecca, their leader, on a white horse. As she passed below me she raised her hand. A row of sooty faces looked up towards me. I heard voices shouting, but they were too far away for me to understand. Were they angry with my father for not joining them?

Or perhaps they thought I was my father. My heart bounded like a stone against my ribs. Perhaps they thought I was going to join them. And why shouldn't I? I was dressed as a woman, wasn't I? And though I wasn't as tall as my father nor as broad, I was tall enough.

In no time at all I was kneeling by the brook and plastering mud on my face. I bundled up my plaited hair on top of my head and tied it with the rag that I'd used to

19

cover my nose. I got the sack from the back of the horse and draped it over my shoulders.

The ground was shaking with the tramp, tramp, tramp of feet as I ran down the hill. The constables at the tollgate must have been shaking too. I could see a small knot of them standing there, but for all Mam's wailing and shouting, there were no soldiers in sight. Those soldiers were probably taking it easy. They never expected Rebecca and her Daughters to attack in broad daylight.

A voice shouted, 'Better late than never,' as I joined the crowd.

A hand slapped me on the back so hard I could feel my plaits jigging on my head. Luckily the rag held firm and I soon stopped feeling scared. Soon all I could think about was waving my fists and shouting and tramping with the rest. I wasn't Lizzie John any more. I was a Daughter of Rebecca.

I could see Rebecca over the heads of the crowd. It was as if she were floating above us all. The sunlight on her feathered hat and white shawl formed a golden cloud.

When that cloud shimmered to a halt, with a lot of bumping and shuffling we all stopped too.

'Shhhhhhhhhh.'

We were still shushing each other, when there came a terrible wail: 'Ohhhhhhhh…'

I jumped and looked at the men around me. They were grinning fiercely and their eyes burned brightly in their sooty faces.

'Ohhhhh!' warbled a high-pitched woman's voice. 'My

poor daughters, my poor mites, what is to become of us?'

'Who's that?' I said hoarsely. 'Who's that speaking?'

No one answered me.

'Who's that speaking?' I asked, clutching the arm of the man next to me.

'It's Rebecca,' he said. 'Who d'you think?' Then he pulled his arm away and shouted out loud, 'Are you all right, Mother?'

'How can you expect me to be all right, my poor child?' Rebecca replied. 'It's the workhouse for us all.'

'Ohhhhhhhh!' moaned the crowd.

Rebecca had got off her horse. I couldn't see her any more, but from a distance her words came to me like a half-remembered dream.

'My poor mites. To think of you all being hauled off to the workhouse. I can't bear it.'

'And whose fault is it, Mother?' asked the crowd with one voice.

'It's that man. He's going to ruin us all.'

When I heard those words, I began pushing my way to the front.

'Shame on him! Shame! Shame!'

'That man, Thomas Bullin, he's only going to get us sent to the workhouse.'

'Yes, Mother. Yes.'

'He's the one who's put this terrible gate across the road to stop a poor old woman going to market.'

'Yes! Yes!'

The crowd had formed a solid wall. Their hot breath

was all around me.

'Did he have any right to put the gate up, my daughters?'

'No, Mother. No.'

'So what do you think we should do?'

'Smash the gates, Mother!'

With a roar the Daughters surged and I was swept away like a stick in a flood. The sack was torn from my shoulders. I was tossed. I was spun. I heard a hammering and a crashing, but didn't see the gate smashed though I felt the remains of it under my feet. When the crowd surged again and spilled across the fields, I stumbled into a ditch and went sprawling.

By the time I'd picked myself up, Rebecca had gone. A man was lying nearby clutching his leg. It was one of the constables. I didn't like the sharp glint in his eye, but I gave him a haughty look before turning away and heading for home.

I hadn't gone half a mile, when I heard footsteps chasing me. I didn't feel so haughty then. Quickly I pulled the rag off my head and tried scrubbing my face. Without the mud I could pretend to be an ordinary girl out walking on the hillside. But the mud was too thick and the rag too small. I threw the rag away, picked up my skirts and ran.

Fast as I ran, those footsteps were gaining on me. What if that constable put me in prison? I was faint with fear and could already hear the prison doors clanging behind me, when a voice rang out.

'Lizzie!' it shouted. ' Lizzie!'

I shuddered to a halt. Running up the hill towards me, all sooty-faced and with a bundle of women's clothes under his arm, was my father. He was even more shocked than I was.

'Lizzie,' he cried, catching hold of my arm. 'You didn't join the crowd at the tollgate, did you? You know this isn't women's work. The Daughters of Rebecca are men, not women.'

'But what about Rebecca herself?' I said, panting.

'What about her?'

'I know who she is.'

No one was supposed to know that. Dad took a step back.

'Who?' he asked.

'Mam,' I said proudly. 'Mam is Rebecca.'

I thought my father would explode then. And he did. All of a sudden he exploded in a huge roar of laughter. Then he turned me round and what did I see in the distance but the furious figure of my mother running towards us with my brothers stumbling after her.

'Your mam has been in the hayfield all afternoon,' he said. 'She isn't Rebecca. I know Rebecca sounded like her, but that's only because the two of them have the same worries.'

I scowled. I didn't like the way he was laughing at me, especially since I'd only joined the crowd for his sake. 'Why should I believe what you say?' I said. 'You broke your promise.'

'I did not,' said Dad. 'I only promised not to go out *tonight* and it's still afternoon.'

'Huh!' I sniffed and turned away. I was angry at Dad and angry because I couldn't understand what was true and what was not. 'Just wait till you tell that to Mam,' I said as I marched off.

A sad high-pitched voice called me back.

'What will become of me then, my poor daughter?' it warbled. 'What will become of me?'

I spun round. Dad was smiling at me with a hat on his head.

Then I understood. I really was Rebecca's daughter.